THE TOWN MOUSE AND THE SPARTAN HOUSE

Terry Deary's Greek Tales

The Town Mouse and the Spartan House

Illustrated by Helen Flook

A & C BLACK
AN IMPRINT OF BLOOMSBURY
LONDON OXFORD NEW DELHI NEW YORK SYDNEY

First published 2007 by A & C Black
an imprint of Bloomsbury Publishing Plc
50 Bedford Square, London WC1B 3DP

www.bloomsbury.com

ISBN 978-0-7136-8221-2

A CIP catalogue for this book is available from the British Library.

Printed and bound in Great Britain by
CPI Group (UK) Ltd, Croydon, CR0 4YY

5 7 9 10 8 6 4

Introduction

Athens, Greece, 430 BC

Aesop the Greek storyteller said:
It is better to eat beans and bacon in peace than cakes and ale in fear.

When I was a boy, I lived in the great city of Athens. It was the finest city in the world and we were the finest people. We were rich.

However, I learned that wealth does not always last. I learned that richness is not always the blessing we think it is. I learned that it is sometimes better to be poor and happy than rich and miserable.

But when I was a boy, I thought we were blessed. Then, one year, it all changed...

It seems the gods of Greece chose to curse us. Our first curse was the Spartan army. The Spartan warriors made their camp outside the city. Every time our army tried to break out, they were driven back or killed.

"Why can't we beat them?" I asked my mother.

She shook her head. "The Spartans are the cruellest people on Earth. They live for war. They are born and grow up to fight and die for Sparta."

“Why do they hate us so much and want to kill us?” I asked.

“Athens is rich. They are jealous. And they worry we will raise an army to attack them. They want to destroy us before we destroy Sparta.”

Every night, my dreams were haunted by visions of their iron swords chopping me slowly into pieces. I was like an Athenian mouse, waiting to be crushed under their heels...

Chapter One

The arrival of the Spartans meant we lived in fear, waiting for them to attack. We could smell the smoke as they burned the farms outside the city walls.

The city was crowded with peasants, who had fled from the fields. The temples were filled with the homeless.

My mother stayed inside.

If she walked down the street, people spat at her.

"I come from Sparta," she explained. "I married your father when we were at peace. Now my country is at war with Athens, the people of the city hate me."

We thought there was nothing worse than the savage Spartans. Then the second curse arrived. The plague...

My father was a doctor and he told me how sickness was spreading through the crowded temples.

"The victims say their heads ache and their eyes go sore," he explained. "They spit blood and vomit. Their bodies are burning and covered in sores. The wretches cannot sleep. In a week they are dead.

"I try to help, but I have no medicines for *this*. All I can do is try to keep the sick away from the ones who are well."

The plague spread from the temples and on through the city. Screaming victims threw themselves down wells to try to cool their fevered bodies.

No one wanted to nurse the sick, and they died in the streets. The bodies were piled high and left to rot. People stole wood, and lit fires to burn their loved ones.

"This is hell," my father said and rubbed his aching head. His eyes grew sore and his body grew fever-hot. He died within a week.

Everyone in Athens had lost a loved one and the streets were filled with weeping. Now we joined them. I cried for my father and I cried for myself. I waited for the plague to take me next. We paid some slaves to take his body to the plague pit.

And then my mother fell ill. Her face glowed with sweat and her fine, dark hair hung tangled and matted on her pillow. Her voice was thin and breathless. "Darius," she said. "Leave the city ... save yourself."

"Where shall I go?" I cried. "The Spartans will capture me!"

"You *are* a Spartan," she whispered. "My brother is a general with the Spartan army. Find him. Find your uncle Alcmaeon."

"But the Spartans are the cruellest people on Earth!"

"Better a live Spartan than a dead Athenian," she told me.

The next day, she died. Our oldest servant, Syme, told me not to cry. "Your mother has joined the gods in the fields of Elysium," he said.

"She's dead!" I sobbed.

"No, she is asleep," he said softly. "When she wakes she will be on the islands of the blessed. Everyone is happy there. She will meet your father again and they will live in peace for ever more."

"And me?" I asked.

"If you live a good life, then one day you will join them there." He smiled. "But for now you must save yourself. Be brave. Remember, your mother's wish was for you to join your Spartan family."

"And you?"

"I'll take my chance in Athens," Syme shrugged. "I am old. The gods will take me if they want, or spare me. I will see your mother has a good funeral. But you must go. And soon."

I didn't wait to be told twice.

I made my plans to run away.

Chapter Two

I wrapped some beans and bacon in a cloth. Food was hard to come by in Athens. Beans and bacon were the best we could do. I looked around the house for something to take with me. Something to remind me of my mother and father. I chose an opal ring that had been my mother's favourite, and a small scroll of my father's, which contained some of his cures for sickness. I tucked it into my belt.

I packed a few clothes and left the house by the first light of morning.

The guards at the walls were leaning wearily on their spears.

"Will you let me out?" I asked.

"The Spartans will get you," one with a sour face sneered. "They will probably use you as target practice for their spears!"

"It's better than dying slowly from the plague," I replied.

The guard shrugged and swung open a small gate in the wall. "May the gods be with you," he said.

But everyone in Athens knew that the gods were with the Spartans.

The Spartan camp was guarded by wide-eyed boys. They were only my age but their eyes were as sharp and hard as spear tips. They grabbed me roughly and tied my hands. They tore open my bundle, ate my food and stole my mother's ring. Then they dragged me into the camp.

"I am Darius ... nephew of Alcmaeon the Spartan," I tried to tell them.

"And I am Brasidas the Spartan," one of the boys laughed. "I am nephew of no one, son of no one."

"You have no parents?"

"Sparta is my mother and my father," he said, his eyes glittering like the sea.

Hard-faced men were loading weapons onto carts and taking down tents. "Are you leaving?" I asked Brasidas.

"We are going back to Sparta to gather in the crops," he explained. "We have helots to do the work – our slaves. But we can't trust them."

"So Athens will be free?" I groaned. Had I left an hour too soon?

"The plague will kill more than Spartan spears," Brasidas snorted. "We'll come back in the spring to take Athens. By then there will be no soldiers left to defend its walls."

He pushed me towards a group of armed men, who were watching the carts being loaded.

"Who's this?" the soldier in the middle of the group asked.

"A spy from Athens, General Alcmaeon," the boy said. "May I hand him over to my company to beat him to death."

The general reached out a massive hand and grabbed Brasidas by the throat. "The boy could be carrying the plague. Why did you bring him into the camp?"

"Sorry, sir, I didn't think!" Brasidas choked.

The general spoke slowly. "Take him away, kill him quickly, and throw his body into the sea."

"Yes, sir," the boy gasped and turned to grab the rope around my wrist.

"Uncle Alcmaeon!" I cried. "I am Darius. The gods will curse you if you kill your sister's son!"

Chapter Three

The general turned and looked at me. "You are the son of Timareta?" he asked.

I nodded eagerly. I think I expected Alcmaeon to wrap his arms around me in welcome.

But the general shook his head wearily. "I have to spare him," he told Brasidas in a cold voice. "Take him back to Sparta as a helot. He can be another pair of hands to gather in the crops. He is in your care now."

My uncle turned away, as if I had never existed. Brasidas pulled at my rope. He set me to work carrying the canvas tents to the carts and unloading them onto the Spartan ships. If I slowed or stumbled, I was beaten with a stick.

Brasidas laughed. "Welcome to the Spartan way of life," he said.

I worked all day in the cruel sun and was given a small bowl of thin porridge. "Fit for a mouse like you," Brasidas said.

The next morning, we set sail.

At home, in Athens, we had had many servants, like Syme, but we hadn't treated them the way the Spartans treated me.

Every day, I worked till I ached. I sat in the stinking water at the bottom of the ship. When the ship leaked, I filled the leather buckets with water, then threw the water over the side.

The ship was old and leaked badly. It seemed I emptied half the ocean over the side. I carried buckets till my arms ached.

When the soldiers had finished eating, I was allowed to feed on their scraps.

At the end of the day, Brasidas took some time to explain the Spartan way to me.

"The greatest crime of all is to run away in battle," he said. "The punishment is death."

"You kill your own soldiers if they try to save themselves?" I asked.

"Life is nothing to a Spartan," he said. "Spartan parents take a new-born baby to be examined by the oldest Spartans. If it looks fit and strong they say, 'Let it live.' If it looks sickly it is taken to the mountains and left to die." He looked at me with pity. "I think a mouse like you would have been left to die."

"But even weak people have their uses!" I argued.

"What?" he jeered.

"I helped my father with his medicines. I could be a doctor when I'm older. I could save lives."

Brasidas nodded. "There was once a Spartan boy who stole a fox cub. When the elders found him, they stood him in front of them. They asked him questions all morning. He said he knew nothing."

"Because they'd punish him?"

"In Sparta, we don't punish someone for stealing, we punish someone for getting caught. That is the only crime. Don't get caught."

"What happened to the boy?"

"At the end of the morning, he fell over. He was dead."

"They killed him?"

"No. He had hidden the fox cub under his tunic and he kept quiet ... even though the fox was eating his guts. That is Spartan bravery."

"That's not bravery ... it's madness! And I don't believe it's true."

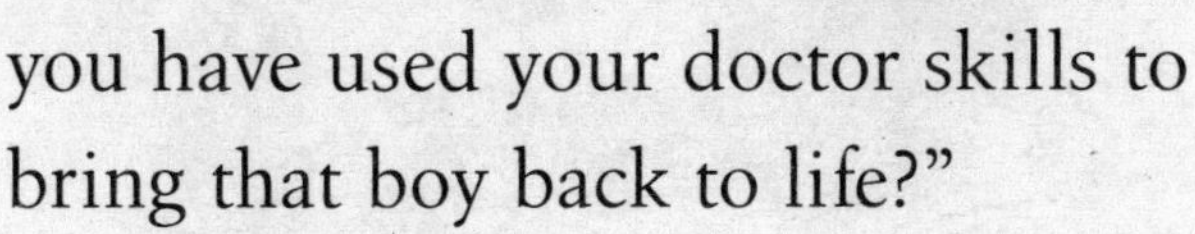

Brasidas looked at me. "What if it *had* been true? Could you have used your doctor skills to bring that boy back to life?"

"No ... but..."

"Then you're worthless. You may as well have been left to die in the mountains."

He stood up and was about to leave when we heard shouts on deck.

"General Alcmaeon is sick ... he is dying!"

Chapter Four

Brasidas groaned. "Alcmaeon is our greatest general. We need him if we are going to defeat Athens."

"I thought you said a Spartan's life is worthless?" I sniffed.

He turned on me furiously with his stick and lashed at my arm. I'd been beaten so much recently, I was used to it and it hardly hurt. Maybe I was starting to become Spartan after all.

"*Some* lives are worthless. A helot like *you* is worthless!"

"So what will you do?" I asked.

"I don't know – our doctors are on one of the other ships. If we wait for them, it may be too late. Alcmaeon would not want to die like this. He would want to die in battle."

"Or maybe he wouldn't want to die at all!" I argued.

Brasidas struck me again. I didn't show the pain.

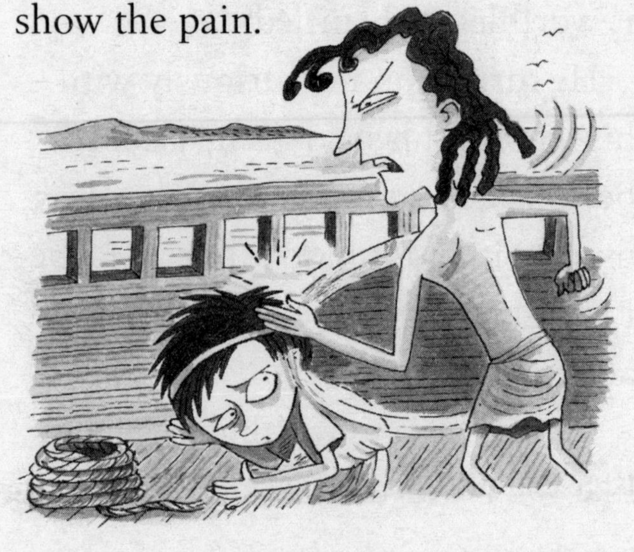

"Maybe we should offer a sacrifice to the gods!" he called down the deck of the ship. "Kill the Athenian boy and scatter his blood on the water!"

The soldiers looked towards me. A few began to nod.

"Wait!" I cried. "The gods are for Sparta. If they want Alcmaeon to die, they will let him die. If they want him to live, they will send him a doctor."

A tall soldier pulled a knife from his belt and waved it under my nose. "Then let's pray to the gods for a doctor. If one doesn't arrive, we'll scatter your blood on the waters!"

The others agreed with a shout. "You are right, Solon!"

Suddenly, I had an idea. "I am a doctor!" I called out.

They turned and looked at me.

I pulled my father's scroll from my belt. "My father was a doctor. He taught me to read his cures. He took me with him to visit the sick. I can cure my uncle Alcmaeon. That's why the gods put me on this ship!"

The soldiers looked uncertain.

They muttered among themselves, then the tall one, Solon, said, "You are wise, young Darius."

"Thank you," I said, with a bow of my head.

"We will let you care for Alcmaeon. You will cure him."

"I'll try," I said brightly.

"No," Solon said. "You will not *try*. You will *succeed*. If you cure Alcmaeon, you will be a hero of Sparta. You will never serve as a helot again."

"That sounds fair," I smiled, and unrolled my scroll.

"It *is* fair," Brasidas said. "But of course if Alcmaeon dies ... then *you* will die, too, Darius."

I stopped smiling.

Chapter Five

I hurried to the cabin at the end of the ship. My uncle lay there, moaning softly. His body was covered in sweat and he had thrown off his tunic. A soldier was holding a wooden bowl at his head.

"Is it the plague?" Brasidas asked.

"It looks like it," I said.

"Then you brought it from Athens!" he raged. "You killed him and you will kill us all. We may as well throw you overboard now."

Solon grabbed Brasidas's arm and stopped him lashing me again.

"I haven't got the plague," I said. "If I had, I would be dead by now. But my father *did* have a cure for it."

I was lying to save my life. I had seen my father at work. One thing he had done to find out why a patient was sick was to look at their vomit. I picked up the bowl. I sniffed it carefully. It smelled of sour dough – of pastry that had turned rotten.

"Has Alcmaeon been eating cakes?" I asked.

Solon nodded. "He is the general. The most important Spartans feast on cakes and ale."

I knew then that Alcmaeon had poisoned himself with rotten cakes. It had been a common illness in Athens in the days before the war. The days when people had fed on cakes and ale. But I was not going to tell the Spartans he was sick from eating bad food.

"Draw me a bucket of water from the sea," I said.

"Why?" Brasidas asked.

I was the doctor now. I turned on him angrily. "Do as I say if you want your general to live," I snapped.

The boy blinked, then hurried off to obey my orders.

When he came back, I said, "Now leave me alone with my uncle."

"You're from Athens," Solon said carefully. "You could kill him!"

I shook my head angrily. "Why would I want to kill him? He is my uncle – if I kill my family, the gods will destroy me. And if he dies, you will feed me to the fishes anyway."

Solon nodded and, taking Brasidas with him, he closed the cabin door.

When they had gone, I raised my uncle's head and began to pour the sea water into his throat. He swallowed weakly. Then he rested. Then he sat up, clutched his stomach and began to retch. The salt water gushed back out of his mouth and nostrils till he was too exhausted to vomit any more.

I let him rest, then gave him the same treatment again. And again.

After the third time, I fed him fresh water and left him at peace. Father's scroll said three times was enough. Three times would clean the stomach of the poison and the patient would live.

Alcmaeon slept. When the morning sun rose over the glittering sea, he opened his eyes and groaned.

Solon hurried into the cabin, "You are alive, General?"

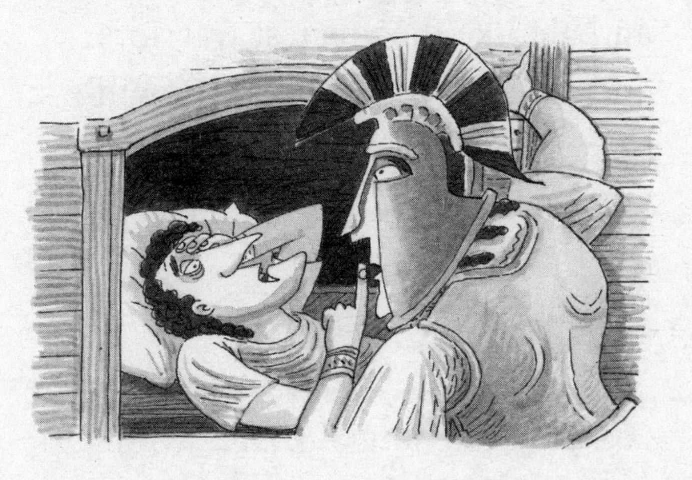

Alcmaeon nodded. "What was wrong with me?"

"You had the plague," I lied. I tapped my scroll. "I am the only person in Athens or Sparta who could cure you."

"You did well, boy," Alcmaeon said and gripped my arm. "You may be an Athenian mouse, but Spartan houses will welcome a hero like you. From now on you will feed on cakes and ale like the greatest warriors and princes. Your every wish will be granted."

"I have just one wish, uncle, just one..." I replied.

Chapter Six

Uncle Alcmaeon set me ashore on the beach at Megara – my wish – and I walked back to Athens. Everywhere, peasants were in the fields, trying to rescue their crops.

"The Spartans have gone!" the gatekeeper told me.

"They will be back in the spring," I said, then wearily I trudged into the city.

I went home and found Syme alive. Smiling, I told him of my adventure and my escape.

"I kept the house safe for you, young Master Darius," he said.

"Thank you, Syme."

"I thought the plague had taken you like your dear parents."

"No, Syme. Father said there are some people who do not catch it no matter how many die around them. I'm one of the lucky ones, as are you."

"What will you do?" he asked.

I pulled out my father's scroll from my belt and looked at the others on the shelves. There were tables covered with his herbs and potions. "I will learn to be a doctor, like my father was," I said. "I think I could be good at it. I cured my uncle and I'd like to cure more people."

Syme smiled. "You're a good lad. Athens needs people like you."

"Sparta *thought* it needed me," I said. Then I laughed. "But they only thought that because they believed I could cure the plague! They promised me a rich life in a Spartan house with cakes and ale. But one day they would have found out the truth ... and they'd have killed me. It's the Spartan way. A cruel way."

Syme shrugged. "We can't offer you cakes and ale ... Athens is a ruined city. We can just manage beans and bacon."

"It may be a ruined city, but it's home," I smiled. "Home."

And I remembered what the storyteller Aesop had said: "It is better to eat beans and bacon in peace than cakes and ale in fear."

Terry Deary's

Greek Tales

The BOY WHO CRIED HORSE

TROY, 1180 BC

Acheron is the best liar in Troy. In his stories he can make King Paris and the Trojan heroes sound like gods. When a stranger arrives in the city, with news that the Greek enemy have left without a fight, Acheron is suspicious. But will anyone believe his latest story?

Greek Tales are exciting, funny stories based on historical events – short chapters and illustrations throughout are perfect for building reading confidence.

ISBN 978 0 7136 8216 8 £4.99

Terry Deary's

Greek Tales

The Tortoise and the Dare

OLYMPIA, GREECE, 776 BC

Ellie is furious – her twin brother Cypselis has made a bet. If he beats Big Bacchiad in the school Olympics foot race, their family will receive a goat, if he loses, she will become the bully's slave. And with the odds stacked against him, how can she make sure Cypselis stands a chance of winning?

Greek Tales are exciting, funny stories based on historical events – short chapters and illustrations throughout are perfect for building reading confidence.

ISBN 978 0 7136 8220 5 £4.99

TERRY DEARY'S

GREEK TALES

THE LION'S SLAVE

SYRACUSE, GREECE, 213 BC

Archimedes is the cleverest man in Greece. So when the Romans attack, everyone believes he'll find a way to save them. Lydia, his slave, thinks so, too, and cheers with the crowd as he creates one amazing invention after another. But who is the *real* brains behind them all?

Greek Tales are exciting, funny stories based on historical events – short chapters and illustrations throughout are perfect for building reading confidence.

ISBN 978 0 7136 8222 9 £4.99